皮皮與波西

♥IREAD
皮皮與波西：小水窪

繪　　　圖	阿克賽爾·薛弗勒
譯　　　者	酪梨壽司

發 行 人	劉振強
出 版 者	三民書局股份有限公司
地　　　址	臺北市復興北路 386 號 (復北門市)
	臺北市重慶南路一段 61 號 (重南門市)
電　　　話	(02)25006600
網　　　址	三民網路書店 https://www.sanmin.com.tw

出版日期	初版一刷 2019 年 1 月
	初版三刷 2022 年 4 月
書籍編號	S858110
I S B N	978-957-14-6541-8

Originally published in the English language as PIP AND POSY:
THE LITTLE PUDDLE
Text Copyright © Nosy Crow Ltd 2011
Illustration Copyright © Axel Scheffler 2011
Copyright licensed by Nosy Crow Ltd.
Chinese translation right © 2016 San Min Book Co., Ltd.

小山丘官網

皮皮與波西

小水窪

阿克賽爾・薛弗勒／圖　　酪梨壽司／譯

小山丘

有一天，皮皮去波西家玩。

他掛好外套，脫下雨鞋。

「我們要玩什麼呢?」
波西問。

他們決定先帶寶貝
玩偶散散步。

接著，他們組了
一大圈火車軌道，
還堆了一個積木小鎮。

玩累了，他們吃個點心休息一下。

皮ㄆㄧ皮ㄆㄧ口ㄎㄡ好ㄏㄠ渴ㄎㄜ啊ㄚ！

吃ㄔ完ㄨㄢˊ點ㄉㄧㄢˇ心ㄒㄧㄣ，皮ㄆㄧˊ皮ㄆㄧˊ和ㄏㄜˊ波ㄅㄛ西ㄒㄧ
玩ㄨㄢˊ起ㄑㄧˇ了ㄌㄜ扮ㄅㄢˋ獅ㄕ子ㄗˇ的ㄉㄜ遊ㄧㄡˊ戲ㄒㄧˋ。

他們吼得太開心，
讓皮皮忘了去尿尿。

忽然間，地板上
出現了一個
小水窪。

喔ㄛ， 天ㄊㄧㄢ啊ㄚ！

「沒關係，皮皮，」
波西說。

「大家都有不小心
的時候。」

波西把她的衣服借給皮皮穿。

之後他們一起畫了好多圖。

皮皮又想尿尿了，
這次他尿在小馬桶裡。

是自己去的喔！

洗澡的時間到了。
浴缸裡有好多好多的泡泡。

太ㄊㄞˋ棒ㄅㄤˋ啦ㄌㄚ˙！

Pip came to play at Posy's house.

He hung up his coat and took off his wellies.

"What shall we play?" said Posy.

First, they decided to take
their babies for a walk.

Next, they built a big
train track and a town.

Then they stopped for a snack.

Pip was **very** thirsty!

And they had such fun **roaring** that
Pip forgot he needed a wee.

After that, Pip and Posy
pretended to be lions.

Suddenly, there was
a little puddle
on the floor.

Oh dear!

"Never mind, Pip,"
said Posy.

"Everyone has accidents
sometimes."

Posy gave Pip some of her clothes to wear.

They spent the rest of the day
painting pictures.

And the next time Pip had to have a wee,
he did it in the potty.

All by himself.

Then it was time for a bath.
With lots of bubbles.

Hooray!

繪者簡介

阿克賽爾·薛弗勒　Axel Scheffler

1957年出生於德國漢堡市，25歲時前往英國就讀巴斯藝術學院。他的插畫風格幽默又不失優雅，最著名的當屬《古飛樂》(Gruffalo) 系列作品，不僅榮獲英國多項繪本大獎，譯作超過40種語言，還曾改編為動畫，深受全球觀眾喜愛，是世界知名的繪本作家。薛弗勒現居英國，持續創作中。

譯者簡介

酪梨壽司

當過記者、玩過行銷，在紐約和東京流浪多年後，終於返鄉定居的臺灣媽媽。出沒於臉書專頁「酪梨壽司」與個人部落格「酪梨壽司的日記」。